A Crabtree Branches Book

SERVING with Honor

COAST GUARD

written by Bernard Conaghan

CRABTREE
Publishing Company
www.crabtreebooks.com

School-to-Home Support for Caregivers and Teachers

This high-interest book is designed to motivate striving students with engaging topics while building fluency, vocabulary, and an interest in reading. Here are a few questions and activities to help the reader build upon his or her comprehension skills.

Before Reading:

- *What do I think this book is about?*
- *What do I know about this topic?*
- *What do I want to learn about this topic?*
- *Why am I reading this book?*

During Reading:

- *I wonder why...*
- *I'm curious to know...*
- *How is this like something I already know?*
- *What have I learned so far?*

After Reading:

- *What was the author trying to teach me?*
- *What are some details?*
- *How did the photographs and captions help me understand more?*
- *Read the book again and look for the vocabulary words.*
- *What questions do I still have?*

Extension Activities:

- *What was your favorite part of the book? Write a paragraph on it.*
- *Draw a picture of your favorite thing you learned from the book.*

Table of Contents

Mission

The United States Coast Guard is a branch of the United States Armed Forces. It is responsible for keeping America's 95,000 miles (153,000 kilometers) of **shoreline** safe.

Values

Guardsmen are expected to live by values. They are honor, respect, and devotion to duty. These core values guide guardsmen's actions every day, whether on or off the job. The Merchant Mariner **Oath** is a promise to follow these values.

Fun Fact

The U.S. Medal of Honor is the country's highest military award. Douglas Albert Munro is the only U.S. Coast Guardsman who has received this honor.

Every service member must say the Oath of Enlistment. Officers say the military oath of office. This is a promise to defend the **U.S. Constitution**.

Uniform

The Coast Guard has strict rules for uniforms. Currently, the Operation Dress Uniform is the basic work uniform. By 2025, it will be replaced by a uniform similar to what Navy sailors wear. All guardsmen must wear the baseball cap. Undress uniforms are for meetings and when going to school.

Fun Fact

Uniforms are called "Trops" or Tropical Blues.

Equipment and Vehicles

Cutters and boats are used by the Coast Guard. The Marine Protector Class Cutter is a patrol boat. The Small Harbor Tug is used for search and rescue. It can also be used for law enforcement.

45-foot (14-meter) Response Boat

Coast Guard Cutter Hamilton

The Coast Guard also uses aircraft for patrol and search and rescue **missions**. The Eurocopter MH-65 Dolphin is a type of helicopter. The CASA HC-144 Ocean Sentry is one airplane also used by the Coast Guard.

CASA HC-144 Ocean Sentry

Eurocopter MH-65 Dolphin

Fun Fact

Big black fins help rescue swimmers swim more powerfully.

One of the most important jobs of the Coast Guard is rescuing boaters. Rescue swimmers wear **dry suits**. They wear strobe lights to be seen by the pilot. Rescue baskets pull the boaters into the helicopter.

Training

Coast Guard members must be strong and ready for missions. Boot Camp is the first type of training. Members learn the values of the Coast Guard. They build physical strength and learn basic skills.

Advance Through Training is next. It is called "A" school. Guardsmen learn skills specific to the job they will do.

Careers

The U.S. Coast Guard has many different types of jobs. Helicopter Rescue Swimmers rescue people during hurricanes. Intelligence Specialists use computers to get information about an enemy or criminal.

Fun Fact

Many jobs in the Coast Guard also prepare guardsmen for jobs as ***civilians****. Some training allows guardsmen to get a professional license from trade organizations.*

The U.S. Coast Guard also has jobs that provide support to the crew. Culinary Specialists prepare and serve the food. Health Services Technicians give medical care.

Keeping equipment working is important. Electronics Technicians repair navigation and communication systems. Machinery Technicians keep all the boats running.

Ways to Serve

There are two main ways to serve in the U.S. Coast Guard. Active duty guardians work full-time. Those in the Coast Guard Reserve serve two days a month and two weeks each year.

Reservist with Coast Guard Sector, Ohio Valley, on patrol during a fireworks show.

Fun Fact

The Coast Guard Auxiliary are civilian volunteers that support the Coast Guard. Some jobs include Marine Safety and Search and Rescue.

The Coast Guard has basic requirements to **enlist**. A person must be a U.S. citizen, between the ages of 17 and 31, and have a high school diploma. The Armed Services Vocational Aptitude Battery (ASVAB) tests a person's knowledge of reading, math, science, and thinking. A military medical exam determines if a person is healthy and strong.

Showing Appreciation

Members of the Coast Guard are on call every day of the year. They put their lives at risk to keep us safe. We celebrate them throughout the year. May is Military Appreciation month.

Thank You

HONORING ALL WHO SERVE

Veterans Day is a time to thank those who are serving. It is also for those who served in the past and are still living. Memorial Day is for remembering the men and women who lost their lives serving their country. Are you ready to serve in the U.S. Coast Guard?

Glossary

civilian (suh·**vi**·lyn) Someone who is not in the armed forces or police

cutter (**kuh**·tr) A light, fast coastal patrol boat

dry suit (**drai soot**) A suit used to block out water

enlist (uhn·**list**) To join the armed forces

mission (**mi**·shn) An assignment

oath (owth) A promise

shoreline (**shor**·lahyn) The line where a body of water and land meet

U.S. Constitution (kaan·stuh·**too**·shn) The rights and laws that are the basis for the government of the United States

Index

Websites

www.uscg.mil
www.gocoastguard.com
www.militaryonesource.mil

About the Author

Bernard Conaghan lives in South Carolina with his German shepherd named Duke. His grandmother was the jeep driver for the Major General for the U.S. Marines during World War II. He is a coach on his son's football team. He always eats one scoop of peach ice cream after dinner.

CRABTREE Publishing Company

Written by: Bernard Conaghan
Designed by: Jen Bowers
Proofreader: Petrice Custance
Print Coordinator: Katherine Berti

Photographs: Cover U.S. Coast Guard photo Petty Officer 1st Class Levi Rea, U.S. flag ©2008 J. Helgason/Shutterstock; p.3 U.S. Coast Guard photo; p.5 Coast Guard photo/Petty Officer 3rd Class Loumania Stewarty; p.6 U.S. Coast Guard photo; p.7 Public domain/PA3 Jamie Bigelow; p.9 U.S. Coast Guard photo; p.10 ©2021 Harun Ozmen/Shutterstock; p.11 U.S. Coast Guard photo; p.12 U.S. Coast Guard photo/Thomas Johnson, U.S. Coast Guard photo/Petty Officer Richard Brahm; p.13 U.S. Coast Guard photo/Lt. Davey Connor, U.S. Coast Guard photo/Petty Officer 2nd Class Thomas M. Blue; p.14 U.S. Coast Guard photo/Petty Officer 1st Class Rob Simpson; p.15 U.S. Coast Guard photo/PA3 David Weydert; p.17 and p.19 U.S. Coast Guard photo/Lt. Natalie Rothman; p.20 U.S. Coast Guard photo/Petty Officer 3rd Class Ross Ruddell; p.21 U.S. Coast Guard photo/Petty Officer 3rd Class Trevor Lilburn; p.22 U.S. Coast Guard photo/Petty Officer 2nd Class Anthony L. Soto; p.23 U.S. Coast Guard photo/Petty Officer 3rd Class Johanna Strickland; p.24 U.S. Coast Guard photo/Petty Officer 3rd Class Tom Atkeson; p.25 U.S. Coast Guard photo/Petty Officer 2nd Class Anthony L. Soto; p.27 ©2019 smolaw/Shutterstock; p.28-29 Black Creator 24/Shutterstock

Library and Archives Canada Cataloguing in Publication

Available at the Library and Archives Canada

Library of Congress Cataloging-in-Publication Data

Available at the Library of Congress

Crabtree Publishing Company

www.crabtreebooks.com 1-800-387-7650

Published in the United States
Crabtree Publishing
347 Fifth Avenue
Suite 1402-145
New York, NY, 10016

Published in Canada
Crabtree Publishing
616 Welland Ave.
St. Catharines, ON
L2M 5V6

Printed in the U.S.A./072022/CG20220201